The

Merdragon

by Frankie Williams & Briannia Dawkins

Art by Briannia "LPAki" Dawkins

In loving memory of Shauntae Dawkins. May your spirit forever live on through the story of Nevaeh.

Special thanks to Jazzmine Dawkins for helping to bring life to The Merdragon, and to Shawn Dawkins for his support.

Chapter 1

Off the Path

I'm sure you've all heard of mermaids and dragons, but let me tell you about Nevaeh. She's a Merdragon, the first and only one of her kind. I know what you're wondering - what **is** a Merdragon? Well, Nevaeh's mother, Zyla, is a mermaid and her father, Volcan, is a dragon.

Coming from royal bloodlines, Nevaeh's parents can both shape-shift - which is something only royals can do. The two met in the forest one day, both had transformed to their human forms - Zyla was picking honeysuckle flowers for its nectar, while Volcan was setting traps for food. They may have met accidentally, but every meeting after that day was planned. The two knew that their people would not accept them being together - so it was kept a secret.

When Nevaeh was born she looked like all the other mermaids, until she started changing. She has the typical mermaid body along with small wings on her back - in between them, a trail of beautiful dragon scales. Nevaeh has bright, orange-red hair that glows at night and dark orange eyes that would also glow at times. Since both of her parents can shape-shift, it's an ability that Nevaeh inherited. As she gets older, she develops new abilities on some of her birthdays. When she turned 5-years-old, wings emerged from her back. This gave her the ability to swim faster than the other mermaids. Other abilities Nevaeh has is being able to breathe fire and become invisible under water.

Although Nevaeh enjoys living with her mother in a beautiful cavern, she loves visiting her father in the volcano he lives in. Her parents wanted her to know both worlds; therefore, Nevaeh spends an equal amount of time with both her parents. When she goes to see her father, she has to shape-shift into her human form - some of her journey is on land. The volcano Volcan lives in houses a small dragon colony. If they were to discover her mermaid side, Nevaeh and her father, despite him being a high ranking general, would be exiled...or worse.

If given the choice to live in the sea or the volcano, Nevaeh would choose the volcano. She's always felt more comfortable in the volcano because there, she could hide who she was and fit in better; in the sea, she could not. The only thing Nevaeh and her mother have been able to hide is her hair that glows at night. Her mother wraps it with kelp and seaweed so no one can see it glowing. Still, during the day, the Merchildren don't accept her because she looks different from them. They tolerate her because her mother is royal and their Merparents make them, but they are not her friends.

When the time comes for Nevaeh to visit her father, she gets excited. This particular morning was no exception.

Shifting from her human form and into a mermaid, Nevaeh jumped into a small pool at the far end of her beautiful chamber - underneath the water rested a spacious cavern. She then swam up to a second opening next to her room's entrance, and pulled herself out of the water.

Emerging within another grand chamber, Nevaeh ran eagerly towards her sleeping mother, Zyla, shouting, "it's time! It's time!"

Stretching and trying to wake up, Zyla joked, "well don't seem so upset about it," and they both burst into laughter.

After eating breakfast, Zyla begins packing Nevaeh's bag for her upcoming journey. The journey to her father takes two days, and her mother travels with her on the first day. They travel together until they reach the place where the land meets the sea, and Nevaeh continues the rest of the trip alone.

"We're almost there. Do you remember the rules?" her mother asked.

Nevaeh looked to her mother, smiled, and said, "One, eat and drink only when I'm hungry or thirsty. Two, stay on course. Finally, three, make sure no one sees me when I shape-shift."

"Good job," Zyla praised.

After many hours of swimming, they finally reached the shoreline. Nearby is a field of wheat that Nevaeh would have to cross to reach the volcano.

At this point, Zyla has come as far as she could go.

She hugs Nevaeh and says, "safe travels, my love, and remember the rules."

"I will mother, don't worry," she responded, hugging her tightly.

Nevaeh dragged her body onto land as far as she could, sliding across the warm sand. She closed her eyes and began swaying to the rhythm of the waves. She takes a deep breath as the springtime breeze picks up, brushing against her cheeks. Nevaeh's body started changing, and within seconds stood a pretty, human girl, with fiery red hair and dark, orange eyes. She then pulled out a beautiful, black dress from her bag and slid it on. Once she's dressed, Nevaeh begins to wave and blow kisses to her mother. She could see that one tear that is always in her mother's eye whenever they parted ways.

Nevaeh started walking until she reached a dirt path through a field of wheat - she would need to cross it to get to the volcano. It would take hours to cross the field, and Nevaeh was already hungry from shape-shifting. She decided to walk a little further so she could eat in a spot she always enjoyed having her lunch. The sound of crying drew near, and Nevaeh cautiously approached. A girl was sitting in the clearing with her head in her hands.

Is that where the crying is coming from? Nevaeh wondered.

The girl was small and petite with black, long, flowing hair. Although she's seen humans before, she never talked to one.

After standing there for some time deciding what to do, Nevaeh said, "hello."

The girl jumped and started backing away, looking up like a deer caught in headlights. Even with a tear-streaked face, you could see that she was a very pretty girl. Her big brown eyes were captivating.

"Are you okay?" Nevaeh asked, cautiously.

"Wh-who are you?" the girl asked through broken sobs, "I've never seen you before."

"I've never seen you before either," Nevaeh replied.

After some thought, the girl, still sniffling, pointed to a forest and said, "my name is Patricia. I live in the town through the trees over there."

Nevaeh looked in the direction Patricia was pointing. Since it wasn't on her course, that was a direction she had never been in.

"Why were you crying?"

"The kids in my town are always mean to me because I'm different," Patricia explained.

Nevaeh looked the girl up and down - she looked like any other human she'd seen.

"Different how?" Nevaeh asked, looking puzzled.

"It doesn't matter. I'd rather not talk about it."

At that moment, Nevaeh and Patricia had the same thought: *If only she knew how different I was.*

Nevaeh was still hungry. She was ready to eat but she didn't want to be rude and eat in front of Patricia, so she offered her some.

"I was about to eat. Would you like some?"

"No thank you," Patricia declined, "I just had lunch a little while ago. But thank you."

Deep down, Nevaeh was a little glad because her mother always packed just enough for her journey. As Nevaeh ate her lunch, the girls talked and laughed. They discovered they liked a lot of the same things. They like to swim, and suck nectar from honeysuckle flowers. They talked for a long time until Patricia jumped up and gasped.

"I forgot I have to meet my little brother, Shaun, at the elementary school and walk him home! Do you wanna come?" She asked Nevaeh.

Nevaeh thought to herself for a moment, *I'm already late, and I broke rule number 2 - but I'm really enjoying my new friend.*

Finally, Nevaeh decided to go with Patricia as long as she was back on her course before it got dark. She couldn't let Patricia see her hair glow.

"Yes, I'll come, but I have to be back here and on my way before dark. I'm going to my father's volca--, uh I mean house."

"Cool!" Patricia beamed, and off towards the town went to the two new friends.

They went through the trees and stepped out into a small town. It was an average town; it didn't appear to be small, but it wasn't too big either. It seemed to be a nice little town that could be easily missed. Venturing deeper into town, Nevaeh's eyes stretched wide as Patricia showed her around. She had never seen so many humans out at one time! They were everywhere and doing all kinds of things. The town bustled with the noise of humans enjoying their morning. The entire town was inviting her in with open arms through the sweet aroma of bread from the local bakery.

"My brother goes to the school over there," Patricia stated as she pointed down the street.

Distracted by the humans, Nevaeh didn't realize she and Patrica had stopped in front of a small building, and was about to go in.

Once Nevaeh noticed, she asked, "what's this?"

Patricia looked at her, confused, and answered, "the store. We're a little early so I thought we could grab a snack."

Patricia held the door open for Nevaeh and walked into the store after her. Nevaeh really wanted to know what a store and a snack was, but decided not to ask. Nevaeh's eyes grew wide as she gazed upon the decorated walls. There are long, wooden shelves that seemingly held an endless supply of items of different shapes and sizes. Nevaeh closed her eyes as she took in the mixture of sweet smells that danced through the air. There were also shelved aisles that held more of these interesting items, well as colorful cans organized like a rainbow.

What is all this stuff? Nevaeh thought.

Nevaeh continued following Patricia around the store, and watching as she picked things up and put them back. Patricia finally settled for two flat things she called, "chocolate." Nevaeh watched curiously as Patricia handed the other human behind the counter something; finally, the two girls walked out of the store. Patricia handed Nevaeh a piece of chocolate, but she didn't know what to do with it. She watched as Patricia tore a bit of the wrapper off and took a bite into the chocolate. Mimicking her, Nevaeh did the same. Once Nevaeh bit into it, she stopped walking and gasped!

"What's wrong?"

Pointing at the candy, Nevaeh asked, "what did you say this was again?"

"Uh, it's chocolate," Patricia chuckled, "you act as if you've never eaten any before."

Nevaeh turned her gaze to the ground, embarrassed, and said, "well…"

A wave of shock washed over Patricia as she exclaimed, "you've never had chocolate!? Here I was thinking my mom is strict."

Trying to change the subject, Nevaeh shoved the rest of the chocolate in her mouth with an, "mmm, tasty."

The girls burst into laughter as they crossed the street, and headed towards the elementary school. Suddenly, a large bell could be heard ringing throughout the town, and it scared Nevaeh. She quickly spun around as her orange eyes began to glow brightly. Luckily, Patricia was looking towards the school and didn't notice Nevaeh's eyes. A large group of excited, human children began rushing out of the school - laughing and shouting. It seemed as if the children were everywhere and coming right for the girls. Nevaeh's eyes grew even brighter, and a small puff of smoke came out of her nose. Patricia was still looking at the school, trying to pick out Shaun from the crowd.

"What do they want," Nevaeh hesitated, "do they want to fight us?"

Patricia laughed as she asked, "fight us? They're just getting out of school. Oh, here comes my brother! Now you'll get to meet him."

Nevaeh was starting to calm down, and the glow in her eyes was fading.

Phew, Nevaeh thought, *that was close.*

Nevaeh learned from her father that her dragon side will come out if she feels threatened or scared. Thank goodness he had also begun teaching her how to control it. Once Nevaeh had calmed herself, she turned towards the direction Patricia was facing, and saw a human that looked like a smaller, boy version of Patricia. As he got closer, he stared confusingly at Nevaeh.

"Who is this?" Shaun asked.

"This is my friend, Nevaeh. Nevaeh, this is my little brother, Shaun."

"She **must** be new in town, because you don't have any friends," Shaun laughed.

Patricia popped Shaun on his bottom, "shut up."

"Ow!" he jumped, "I'm telling mom!"

"Well if you do, I guess I'll just have to eat this piece of chocolate. A real shame, because I saved it just for you."

Patricia teased Shaun as she waved the piece of candy around his face like a pendulum. His eyes followed, almost as if mesmerized.

"Okay, okay," he caved, licking his lips, "I won't tell."

Patricia handed Shaun the chocolate, and Nevaeh watched as he began to eat it. She wanted to grab the piece of chocolate and throw it in her mouth, **badly**. Nevaeh was glad she'd been taking self-control lessons from her father. The girls talked and laughed, while Shaun was enjoying his chocolate, as they walked deeper into town. Catching the sweet scent of chocolate with every breath, Nevaeh couldn't help but glance in his direction from time to time. Nevaeh could smell really well, and her nostrils flared in excitement from the scent.

Mmm, Nevaeh thought.

She'd been inhaling the smell so deeply, she didn't notice they had stopped in front of a pretty, blue and white house.

"What are we getting from this store," Nevaeh began to ask, "more chocolate?"

"This is not a store," Patrica answered, "this is my house."

Nevaeh had never seen where humans lived. Until today, she had never even talked to a human. Suddenly, a human woman came out of the house, holding her arms out in Shaun's direction - he happily ran to her.

"Did my big boy have a big boy day?" Asked the woman in an adoring tone.

Shaun happily started giving details about his day.

The woman then noticed Nevaeh, and asked, "And who is **this** young lady?"

"Her name is Nevaeh," Patricia answered, "and she's my new friend!"

The woman seemed to make a strange face at first; she'd never met anyone Patricia might have called her friend.

"It's nice to meet you, Nevaeh," she finally responded, "I'm Patricia and Shaun's mother, Lillie. Are you new to town?"

"Yes ma'am, I am," Nevaeh answered.

"Oh," Lillie raised an eyebrow, "so, where do you live?"

"Mom," Patricia whined, "can you please not ask her 100 questions?"

Nevaeh was glad Patricia cut in - she had no answer.

"Do you think it would be okay if Nevaeh and I hung out a little while longer," Patricia begged.

Lillie thought for a moment and said, "as long as you get home before dark, I guess it's okay."

"Thanks, mom," Patricia exclaimed.

The two girls turned away, but just as they began walking Nevaeh stopped.

"Oh no!" She exclaimed.

" 'Oh no' what?"

"I'm supposed to be headed to my father's house, and I'm going to be so late!"

Concerned, Patricia asked, "Is your dad going to be mad?"

"I don't know," Nevaeh thought for a moment, "I've never been late before. I'd better head back to the field. It takes **hours** to cross."

"Oh, okay," Patricia said, obviously saddened, "then I'll walk with you."

Delighted that she volunteered, Nevaeh agreed. They headed out of town in the direction of the field, talking and laughing as they walked. Then, almost out of nowhere, Nevaeh spotted a snake just a few feet ahead to the left. Having been taught numerous lessons by her parents, she recognized it to be a poisonous snake. Patricia, on the other hand, didn't notice it and continued.

Nevaeh knew that she couldn't let Patricia get any closer because it was way too dangerous.

Suddenly, an idea popped into Nevaeh's head.

She pointed in the opposite direction and said, "Hey, what's that over there?"

"What?" Patricia said, turning to look as her ears wiggled slightly.

When she turned, Nevaeh blew a small stream of fire and singed the snake. This startled it, causing it to hiss violently as it slithered deep into the wheat. Eyes squint, Patricia was still looking off into the distance for whatever Nevaeh had pointed to.

She turned to Nevaeh, finally asking, "what did you see? I don't see anything."

"Oh, it must have just been some kind of animal."

"Well, whatever it was, it's gone now."

"Yeah," Nevaeh responded, glancing at the scorched spot the snake fled from, "it is now."

As the girls continued their travels through the field, a thought occurred to Nevaeh.

"Hey, you're walking me to the end of the field, but it will be dark on the way back to your town, right?"

"Yeah," Patricia answered, "but it'll be fine."

Nevaeh was starting to feel bad that she let Patricia accompany her. She wanted to walk her halfway back home. However, Nevaeh knew that by the time they would reach the halfway mark, her hair would be glowing - she couldn't let Patricia see.

Seeing the concern on Nevaeh's face, Patricia assured, "really, I'll be fine. Don't worry."

Patricia then smiled at her to try and make her feel better...but it wasn't working. They continued walking for what felt like forever. Finally, they reached the end of the field and could see the volcano off in the distance; Patricia looked curiously at Nevaeh.

"So, just **where** does your dad live anyway?" Patricia continued, "I thought the volcano was the only thing out there."

"No, no, there's a town over that way," Nevaeh pointed.

Patricia twisted her face in confusion, "but I've never seen a town out there."

"Well, I've never seen your town before today either."

The girls looked at each other for a moment, then burst into laughter.

"Right," they said in unison, causing them to laugh harder.

"Well," Nevaeh started, "I guess you need to head back. It **will** be getting dark soon."

"I can walk you out a little more."

"No!" Nevaeh blurted in a panicked voice, trying to keep her cool.

"I don't mind. Besides, I already told you I would be okay," Patricia insisted.

"This really is far enough. I'm fine from here, and it's not much further."

"Well, how long are you going to be at your dad's house? I could meet you here and we can hang out for a little while."

"I'll be back here in 14 days," Nevaeh replied.

With that said, the girls looked off into the direction of the volcano.

"I guess I need to get started, I'm already late and don't want to be any later."

As she said this, Nevaeh turned back to look at Patricia, who was no longer there.

"She was just right here…" Nevaeh looked out across the huge field.

She wanted to look for her new friend, but she was already late. It was getting darker and her hair was beginning to glow. Nevaeh could only hope Patricia was okay as she continued to the volcano.

Meanwhile, inside the volcano, a feeling of unease loomed over the dragons. They seemed bothered, because they were all assembled and in their human forms.

Unlike other races, where only those of royal bloodlines can shape-shift, all dragons can. There are no kings and queens of dragons, only the Ancient Ones, and all dragons share their blood. While inside the volcano, their human skin takes on a greenish hue and is extremely thick to protect them from the heat. Attached to their body are thin, rough scales that resemble clothing. Each dragon has a unique layout of scales. However, outside of the volcano, during the day, their skin takes on a more natural, human skin tone - their scales are no longer visible. The humans have always kept their distance, making it easy for the dragons to go undetected for so long. Humans avoid the volcanoes for fear of lava - which is actually dragon spit.

The volcano has many cave pockets so that each dragon has their own, smaller cave. The Ancient Ones' quarters are near the top of the volcano. They often stand out in front of their quarters and watch over the colony. At this moment, not a single dragon was in their den, and the Ancient Ones were looking upon their brethren.

"We will search by air, and land until we find her!"

All eyes were on a man who stood about six-feet-tall, standing in the center of the others. His bulky muscles flinched as he spoke - the tension in his body could be seen. His dark, red hair and eyes were glowing brighter as he spoke - this is Volcan.

He turned to the only two dragons left in their original forms and ordered, "Drakon, Beakon, you two will search overhead."

He then turned towards one other dragon in her human form, "Veara, you will fly to our sister volcano and check there."

"Yes, sir," Veara sternly responded.

"We will not rest until she's here and safe."

Upon hearing this, everyone divided into various groups and started positioning themselves.

As this was going on, Nevaeh was standing on a cliff attached to the volcano.

This is close enough, she thought.

She slipped off her dress and swiftly hid it under some rocks. Nevaeh then started swaying back and forth as she'd done earlier. Within seconds, a golden-brown dragon now stood in her place. It had orange eyes and an orange cowlick of hair on its forehead. Nevaeh had fully morphed into her dragon form.

She flew towards the mouth of the volcano, and, looking down, instantly noticed the large crowd gathering.

I wonder what's going on, she pondered.

Nevaeh then saw her father, Volcan, in the center of the floor and decided to land beside him. Once landed, she shifted to human and looked around at the other dragons.

"What's going on, father?"

Chapter 2

Into the Volcano

"Wow" Patricia exclaimed, "I think I broke my own record. I'm pretty sure I crossed the field in 20 minutes!"

Normally, the average person walking the field would take a little over two hours. However, Patricia is not the average person - she is a Deerling. Her mother, Lillie, is a human. Her father, Azar, is a royal Buck with the ability to shape-shift.

Lillie stumbled upon Azar one day in the woods, when she went on a hunting trip, and a spotted a buck caught in a food trap. She took aim at the buck with her shotgun - ready to take him home to prepare him for dinner that night. The huge buck stopped struggling to get out of the trap, and stood there gazing at Lillie. Something about its eyes captivated her, causing her to lower her weapon. Lillie began talking in a soothing voice while moving towards it. Strangely enough, the buck stood there and watched as she crept closer to unclasp the trap. Once free, Lillie expected the buck to run off, but it stood there instead.

Suddenly, in place of the buck stood a man, Azar. He stood to up 6-feet tall, with flowing, black hair. His black eyes were captivating, and Lillie rubbed her eyes in disbelief as she stared upon them.

"What…are you?" Lillie murmured.

Azar started talking in a soothing yet powerful voice.

"Thank you for sparing my life, and setting me free."

"I'm sorry," Lillie looked at him, confused, "I don't understand what's going on."

Azar explained to her that he was a Buck who could shape-shift into a human, and lived among a race called Deerling.

"I am a prince among my people," he explained.

They sat in the woods and talked for hours. After that day, they began meeting daily and going for long walks. Before they knew it, the two had fallen in love.

One day, Lillie told Azar she was with child. He volunteered to leave his kingdom and live with Lillie in her town. However, Lillie didn't want to make Azar choose between her, his duties as a prince, and the future king of his people. He knew she'd never be accepted by his people, so they came up with a plan.

Patricia would live with her mother but upon her 15th birthday - two years from now - she would be introduced into the Deerling world. Azar would not interfere with her growing up until then. Once Patricia was born, Lillie would meet him every day so that he could spend time with his daughter. During these times, Azar would also tell Lillie things Patricia would experience as she got older. Azar wanted to prepare her on how to deal with them. Their meetings stopped when

Patricia turned 2-years old as Lillie and Azar didn't want her to question her origins.

As Patricia got older, she started noticing things about herself, one of which was being able to hear quite well. Well enough to where she could hear people from a great distance. She shared this with her mother who, thanks to Azar, managed to teach her how to control this ability.

Whenever Patricia asked her mom how she knew what to teach her, she would just say, "one day I'll tell you."

During school, Patricia was able to hear a couple of girls from her class in the locker room planning a prank on her. They planned to throw a small bucket of water on Patricia as soon as she walked in.

As she got closer to the locker room, she heard a voice say, "she's coming."

Patricia then stopped and decided to get the assistant principal, Mrs. Henderson. Patricia claimed she needed help with her locker. As soon as the two walked into the locker room--

SPLASH!

Mrs. Henderson was soaked by the bucket of water instead of Patricia, causing the girls to get sent to the principal's office. Several backfired pranks later, the kids were convinced Patricia was weird and decided they'd no longer talk to her.

Later that day, after she'd gone home, something happened. Patricia and her mother were home alone when she let out a deafening scream from the bathroom, causing her mom to drop the dishes she was putting away. Lillie ran to check on Patricia, screaming, "what's wrong?" as she flung the door open.

Lillie slapped her hand over her mouth, half surprised at what she was seeing. In the middle of the bathroom floor lay a panicking Patricia, the top half of her human but the bottom half a deer body. Lillie could see the fear in her daughter's face - Patricia didn't know what was happening; Azar had warned this would happen one day. Lillie, remembering what he'd said to prepare her for this day, calmed Patricia down by talking to her in a soothing voice while softly looking into her eyes. Several minutes later in the spot Deerling Patricia once laid now stood a human Patricia, her legs back to normal.

"What's going on, mom? What's happening to me?" she sobbed.

"Keep calm," Lillie reassured her, "I'm going to explain as much as I can to you right now."

Lillie began telling Patricia about all the things that made her different from the other kids. Her mother explained what made her special, and also told her that it must be kept a secret between them.

Soon after she was done explaining, Patricia asked, "is Shaun like me?"

"No, but as I said, soon you will know everything…just not today."

Lillie then began explaining to her how to control her shape-shifting powers with the knowledge Azar had given to her.

I'm going to have to tell Nevaeh about me, Patricia thought as she trotted out of the field and headed towards town.

Getting a good distance towards the town, Patricia was about to shape-shift back to a human when she began to feel a harsh pressure on both her shoulders. Patricia winced as the pain got more intense and she felt her body being lifted off the ground. Now terrified, Patricia saw her little Deerling legs dangling in the wind as she noticed the ground getting further away. She was lifted so high, she could see the entire town. She looked up to see what had grabbed hold of her, but all she could make out was darkness.

" 'What's going on' is we were about to search for you," Volcan exclaimed, shooting Nevaeh a stern look as his eyes began to glow brighter.

"Why, father?"

"We dragons are creatures of habit. When you were not on time, we assumed you were in danger," Volcan sighed, "this is why there are rules and you must follow them…always."

Nevaeh hung her head down saying, "I'm sorry, father."

The glow in Volcan's eyes began to fade.

"All is forgiven, just remember to honor the rules."

Just then two child voices called out to Nevaeh; it was her friends, Zander and Ayla, sprinting towards her.

"Why were you so late!?" the two asked in unison.

"Did you miss me?" Nevaeh replied mockingly.

The three children began to laugh. Nevaeh hugged her father, then ran off with her friends to get caught up.

Patricia had an alarming thought, *What's going on!? Where is this thing taking me!?*

She could now see the volcano coming into view, and they seemed to be flying towards it. As they crept closer she realized they were not only going towards the volcano, they were going **in** it! Patricia was afraid both her and whatever was holding her were going to burn up, but once they were inside she was surprised at the sight. There were dozens, no, hundreds of caves lined along every inch of the walls, and inside of the volcano itself was surprisingly bright. Patricia saw many things walking around on the ground, but was too high up to make out what they were. She decided to look up to see what was holding her, and she couldn't believe it.

"A dragon!?" she sputtered, "Is this real!?"

Just as she looked at it, Patricia felt its grip loosen on her and she began to fall. Her fall was broken, with whatever she landed on producing a squishy sound. Patricia lifted herself to her feet while gripping the jagged rocks along the walls, and turned back to her human form in order to keep her balance. She looked around and realized she'd been dropped into some kind of deep pit. She saw all types of creatures inside the pit with her, but she couldn't understand what was going on and why she'd been carried off. As Patricia stared with wonder and confusion towards the opening above her, she noticed a pair of eyes staring back down at her. Making out that it appeared to be a human child, she began waving both her arms towards it.

"Hey," Patricia shouted, "where am I? Could you help me get out of here?"

The figure just stared back at her and said, "sorry, but I'm not allowed to play or talk with food."

Soon after, the child's gaze on her vanished as it ran from the opening of the pit.

"Food? What do they mean by 'food?' Are we…food!?"

Nevaeh and her friends were talking and laughing when she looked up, noticing a large man was watching her from above. It was Vavlar, one of the Ancient Ones of the colony. He stood between 7 and 8-feet tall as he glared at her with his burgundy eyes. He was the kind of dragon whose voice was so deep that when he raised it, the volcano trembled as he spoke. As Nevaeh looked back at him she bowed her head in his direction as she'd been taught to do to show respect. However, he simply stared back at her with a disapproving, yet intimidating, glare. Nevaeh began to slowly turn away, continuing the conversation she'd been having with her friends.

"There's something off about that girl," Vavlar grumbled to himself.

The Ancient Ones shared a connection to all the dragons in the colony, but Vavlar felt no such connection with Nevaeh. This made him suspicious, wondering where she would disappear to for 14 days at a time. Vavlar had spoken to Volcan about her constant disappearances.

"She lives in our sister volcano with her mother," Volcan lied.

At the time, Vavlar accepted his explanation. However, his suspicions had reemerged and he continued to watch Volcan and Nevaeh closely.

"I wonder what the others gathered for our meal tonight," Ayla pondered as she looked at Nevaeh and Zander.

"How about we go take a peek?" Nevaeh replied.

The three children walked towards the pit at the far right of the cave to take a look at the food inside. As they poked their heads over the opening, Nevaeh's eyes widened in shock as she jumped back.

Patricia? she thought.

Nevaeh? About the same time Nevaeh had poked her head over the opening, Patricia looked up and saw her.

Or at least she thought she saw Nevaeh. Before Patricia could get a good look at the girl, Nevaeh ducked out of view.

Nevaeh began to briskly walk away from the pit, nearly to the point of running, trying to process whether or not her eyes were deceiving her.

"I'm getting so hungry, just looking at all that food is making it worse," Ayla groaned, her and Zander not realizing Nevaeh walked away as they continued staring into the pit.

"Hey, it was your idea."

"Well, I couldn't help it," Ayla groaned.

"Wait a minute," Zander said looking back at Nevaeh, who was now sitting on the other side of the volcano with her head in her hands.

"What's wrong?" Ayla asked as the two of them walked over and sat down beside Nevaeh, startling her.

"Nothing," Nevaeh stuttered, "I was just wondering what I missed while I was gone."

"Oh, is that all? We can fill you in on that," Ayla laughed.

Nevaeh's friends began talking to her, informing her of all the things that had been going on in the volcano while she was away for 14 days. They also giggled as they talked about how all the dragons were scurrying around on high alert when she was late. As they discussed, Nevaeh occasionally nodded to make it seem like she was listening, all while casting glances at the pit. She was sure she saw Patricia in the pit, and began to plan on how she would save her new friend. She knew she had to do something before dawn. After all, that's when all the dragons would gather at the pit to eat before heading to sleep. As Nevaeh zoned in on what her friends were saying from time to time, Vavlar continued to watch the girl from above.

"Something's just not right," he said one last time before submerging into the shadows of his cave.

When the feeling of being watch returned to Nevaeh, she knew she had to be extra careful if she wanted any chance of saving Patricia. She looked up to the sky through the mouth of the volcano - mealtime was approaching. For several minutes, Nevaeh played the plan she thought up over and over again. Suddenly, her thoughts were interrupted by the sound of a thunderous voice from above.

"It is time," it was Vavlar, causing the volcano to tremble as he spoke even while still in his cave.

Suddenly, all the dragons began shifting from their human forms into dragons, and making their way to the center of the volcano to wait - everyone, but Nevaeh. In her dragon form, Nevaeh snuck her way past the outskirts of the large group and into the shadows by the food pit. She reached her arm into the pit and, with one large motion, scooped Patricia up and brought her closer to her face. Terrified, Patricia opened her mouth to scream, but Nevaeh took her index claw up to her mouth as if to say, "shh." Patricia swallowed her scream and stared into the dragon's eyes; for some reason, she no longer felt threatened. Patricia scanned the cave, growing wide-eyed as she looked upon the large group of dragons. At any moment, one of them could turn around and see her. Before she could react, Patricia was grabbed and was now underneath Nevaeh. Nevaeh then lowered her wings and tail so that no one could see under her.

Nevaeh began creeping through the shadows the best she could with Patricia crawling beneath her. Nevaeh looked around to check if anyone had seen her, but the dragons hadn't noticed. Nevaeh was so close to her cave now - just a few feet left.

"Hey, you," a voice called out to Nevaeh from the crowd of dragons.

She turned around and saw it was her father, tramping over to her.

"What are you doing over here, we're about to start eating."

Nevaeh was frozen in fear, trying to think of an excuse.

"I just need to head to my cave real quick, I'll be back," she answered.

Volcan sighed, he was trying to figure out what Nevaeh was up to. Just before he could question her, Vavlar's voice rang out through the volcano once again as he flew his way down to the center.

"Now, we eat," Vavlar shouted, causing the dragons to roar in excitement.

Volcan looked at Nevaeh, he really wanted to know what she was up to.

Instead, he just looked at her and said, "alright, but hurry back," as he headed off to the group that formed a line in front of the food pit.

Nevaeh breathed a sigh a relief, her heart nearly jumped out of her chest. There was no time to relax now, she had to get Patricia into the cave before anyone else decided to stop her. She began crawling towards her cave once again, Patricia crawling underneath her. Finally, making it inside, she let Patricia crawl from under. Nevaeh gestured towards a large boulder in the corner of the nearly barren den. Patricia looked at the boulder, then back at the dragon, and somehow understood that she needed to hide behind it. Once she was well hidden, Nevaeh turned around towards her cave entrance and peeked out. She noticed that everyone was now chomping together in the center of the volcano. She quietly crept out of her cave, picked out whatever morsels were left in the pit, and joined the other dragons.

"What is that girl up to?" Vavlar asked himself as he finally looked up from his meal.

He could have sworn Nevaeh wasn't in the circle before, but there she was eating as if she'd always been there. Still suspicious, he was quite hungry so he didn't bother questioning it further.

The sun was beginning to peek above the horizon as the morning approached, signaling that it was time for the dragons to go to sleep for the day. Everyone was finishing up their food, and some had even made their way back to their caves to sleep - including Vavlar. Nevaeh tried to enjoy her meal, but couldn't as she was constantly making sure no one would stumble upon Patricia.

She gobbled down her meal quicker than she'd ever done before, kissed her father good morning, and went off towards her cave. Nevaeh tip-toed quietly towards her bed made of straw, flowers, and grass as she noticed

Patricia had dozed off behind the boulder. Nevaeh couldn't sleep, she had to stay awake to make sure all the dragons were asleep before she could enact the rest of the plan.

A bit of time passed as Nevaeh had been checking over her shoulder from time to time. The dragons had finally cleared out and went into their caves. Nevaeh poked her head out and looked around to make sure everyone had gone to sleep for the day.

"5 more minutes," said Patricia in a drowsy voice as Nevaeh attempted to wake her up.

After giving her a slightly harder shove, Patricia's eyes finally popped open as she remembered where she was. She almost screamed until she saw the dragon that saved her, and she calmed down instantly. Patricia crawled under Nevaeh as she'd done earlier, and they crept out of the cave.

Upon hearing a noise from below, Vavlar awoke from his slumber. Stretching out his talons, he rose to his feet. He then peeked over the edge of his cave and down to the center of the volcano. At first, he didn't see anything, but then Vavlar noticed Nevaeh hunched over. Nevaeh was in an awkward position as she slowly made her way out of the cave. He wasn't able to see Patricia due to his overheard view. Vavlar watched as Nevaeh began to gently flap her wings as to not wake up the other dragons. Then, as fast as lightning, she lifted herself and Patricia, and swooped past Vavlar out the mouth of the volcano. She'd gone so fast he didn't notice she was carrying anyone.

"Now where are you going at a time like this?" he asked himself, taking off after her.

As Nevaeh flew through the sky, Vavlar kept his distance so she wouldn't see him.

Humans are so strange, Nevaeh thought to herself as she looked down.

Though there was barely any sunlight pouring across the land, there were still a few humans up going about their business as birds sang their morning tune. She didn't expect to see anyone this early into the day. To avoid being seen by them, Nevaeh began flying through the clouds. The fact that the morning fog hadn't yet lifted helped mask the girls.

"This isn't the direction of our sister volcano…" Vavlar said to himself as he tried to keep up.

Though he'd been following Nevaeh's every move, the clouds and fog had been hitting him in the face making it hard to see anything.

We're almost there, Nevaeh thought to herself as the wheat field came into view.

She then dove down out of the clouds and landed without Vavlar noticing. After some time of flying, he finally realized that Nevaeh had suddenly vanished as he could no longer see her.

"Drats, where did she go?" he grumbled, but no matter how hard he looked he could no longer find Nevaeh in the clouds.

He decided to give up and head back to the volcano where he planned on questioning her.

Patricia almost fell to the ground as the dragon let her go, she was so shaken she could barely stand. She looked around and realized something.

"I'm in the field near my town," she said as she looked at the dragon, "how did you--"

Before she could finish her sentence, the huge dragon started to change in front of her. Before her eyes now stood Nevaeh.

"Nevaeh? How…what?" Patricia couldn't form any sort of cohesive sentence, so Nevaeh chimed in.

"Sorry I didn't say anything earlier, but I had to get you out of there!"

"No, no, it's okay. I have something to show you, too!"

Patricia then closed her eyes and began whispering to herself. Suddenly, before Nevaeh now stood Patricia in her Deerling form. Patricia's upper body was human, and her lower body that of a deer. She quickly turned back to a human without saying another word. The two girls simply stared at each other. Though no words were exchanged, they both understood each other a little better. The two of them hugged.

"Thank you," Patricia broke the silence.

"Always," Nevaeh said through a smile.

The girls talked some more, but only for a short amount of time as they both needed to get back home. Nevaeh looked back at the volcano as Patricia looked to her town in the distance.

"Will you still be waiting for me in 14 days?" Nevaeh asked.

"I'll be right here."

The two girls hugged once again as they turned and headed their separate ways. Patricia began to walk off when she felt a large gust of wind. She turned around, and there was Nevaeh as a dragon flying off.

"Wow…a dragon," she stared at her friend in disbelief.

"You're late," said Lillie as Patricia walked into the house. She was sitting at the dinner table with three plates in front of her.

Two were empty, while one, Patricia's, was a full plate of food.

"Where were you? You had me worried sick," Lillie said as she collected the two empty dishes, and put them into some dishwater that had grown cold overnight.

"I lost track of time. It was so dark that Nevaeh asked if I wanted to say the night at her place."

"So you walked back here alone?"

"Sorry," Patricia held her head down.

Lillie sighed, saying, "it doesn't matter. So long as you're back safe. What did you have for dinner?"

"I almost was dinner," Patricia mumbled under her breath.

"What was that?"

"Oh, nothing. I'm actually pretty sleepy. I'm heading up," Patricia answered.

"At this time? But it's such a nice morning," Lillie said as she began opening the blinds above the sink. The fresh sunlight poured into the kitchen.

"I didn't exactly get enough sleep at Nevaeh's place," Patricia said as she grabbed the plate from the table and stuck it in the fridge.

"Well then, 'goodnight,' " her mother said playfully.

"Goodnight, mom," Patricia laughed.

Nevaeh was flying as fast as she could, trying to get back to the volcano before she was missed all while making sure no humans saw her. Finally, the volcano had come into view. As soon as her feet touched the ground she shifted back into her human form.

"Phew, made it."

Nevaeh dragged her feet as she made her way toward her cave. She was exhausted and could not wait to plop down onto her nest to catch some sleep. Just as she made it to the entrance of her cave, Vavlar stepped out from the shadows. He was now blocking her path.

"And just where did you run off to?" he asked.

"Uh, I went out to get some air. It was just so stuffy in here and…"

"So you chose to go out at a time when the humans could have easily spotted you? Not only that but so far, too," Vavlar began to stroke his chin.

"Well, I just wanted to--."

"I also could have sworn you weren't present at the beginning of mealtime."

Hearing the commotion, Volcan walked out of his cave while stretching.

"What's going on here?"

"Well," Vavlar began, "your daughter seems to have left the volcano claiming she went to 'get some air.'"

Volcan looked at him confusingly, then looked at the sky and said, "with all due respect, Vavlar, it seems she was only out for mere minutes. I do believe she has not broken any rules either."

Vavlar stepped up to Volcan, his eyes beginning to glow. For a moment, it seemed as if they were about to come to blows. Though Vavlar was angry, he knew he didn't have any evidence of Nevaeh's wrongdoing.

"This one," he pointed towards Nevaeh, "this one does strange things. I will be watching."

Vavlar shot Nevaeh and Volcan one last look before turning into a dragon and flying upward to his cave.

Volcan waited a few seconds to make sure that Vavlar had actually left.

"Be careful of him." he warned, "Rest well, little one, we have a lot of lessons to cover."

Nevaeh hugged her father and they both returned to their caves to sleep.

For the next 14 days, Nevaeh enjoyed playing with her friends and training with her father. Her main objective was to stay out of Vavlar's way; however, Nevaeh could feel him watching her while she pretended not to notice.

Chapter 3

Secrets Revealed

Although Nevaeh loved the volcano more than the sea, she anxiously waited as the time to go home finally crept up on her. For several days Nevaeh had to deal with the sensation of Vavlar's gaze burning the back of her neck - she was tired of being watched. It seemed as if he was everywhere she looked. Vavlar watched Nevaeh from the shadows while she went around saying her goodbyes to her friends. Nevaeh peeked inside her father's cave and waved in his direction; he was adding extra straw and bones to his nest.

"I'm ready to leave, father," she called out to him.

He turned around, smiled, and walked out of the cave. They both walked towards the center of the volcano. As they entered, the moonlight showered down on them.

"Okay," Volcan rested his hand on Nevaeh's shoulder, "do you remember the rules?"

"Yes."

"Now do you understand why you should break none of them?"

Nevaeh hung her head down in embarrassment, remembering how the dragons reacted to her tardiness, and said, "Yes, father, it will never happen again."

With that, the two of them hugged each other. Nevaeh shifted into her dragon form, began flapping her wings and lifted herself off the ground. Not realizing Vavlar was close by, Volcan watched as his daughter quickly made her way out of the volcano's mouth. Nevaeh made it outside and landed on the cliff's edge where the dress was hidden. She dug through the rubble with her claws, made sure no one was watching, and snatched up her dress before flying away. Nevaeh had to hurry if she wanted to make it over the field before sunrise.

After Volcan returned to his cave, Vavlar snuck out of his hiding spot, shifted to a dragon, and flew outside of the volcano. After Vavlar looked around, he caught a glimpse of Nevaeh flying off at a distance.

"Ah, there you are," Vavlar rubbed his claws together, "time to see where you're really going."

Vavlar moved through the sky at a great speed - he ducked through the clouds to make sure she didn't spot him.

"I will find out where this strange one is going," he said with a smirk, "if it's the last thing I do."

Promising to meet at the clearing they'd first met, Nevaeh had reached the destination and saw Patricia waiting. Nevaeh landed, shifted to her human form, and quickly slid into her dress. Landing in the nearby field of wheat, Vavlar managed to land close by, shifting into his human form.

"Welcome back." Patricia greeted.

Nevaeh waved and walked over to her. The two girls laughed and hugged each other.

Hmm, why does that black-haired human look familiar? What's going on here? Vavlar thought to himself as the girls interacted.

Patricia and Nevaeh began immediately talking about what had happened at the volcano two weeks ago. They now knew how different each other were, and it seemed to bond them together. As the two walked through the field, Vavlar slowly followed them. Nevaeh decided she would tell Patricia about her mermaid side. After all, Patricia trusted Nevaeh enough to show her Deerling side.

Nevaeh watched in amusement as the expression on Patricia's face changed when she said, "you know, I'm also a mermaid."

"What!?" Patricia shouted, but barely in disbelief.

With all that had happened lately, she was willing to believe what Nevaeh said as the truth, without hesitation.

"How can you be a human, dragon, **and** a mermaid? I wish I were that lucky."

With a big smile on her face, Nevaeh began laughing as Patricia continued rambling enthusiastically. After Patricia calmed down, Nevaeh began telling the story she'd heard from her parents about how they met. Patricia listened closely as her eyes seemed to grow wider. She was too intrigued to even think about looking away.

"So, that's how I am what I am." Nevaeh proudly proclaimed.

She looked towards the sky, "it looks like it's almost time for me to meet my mother."

The sun had risen slightly as the girls were now almost out of the field.

Patricia clasped her hands together and asked, "does that mean I'll be able to meet your mom?"

Nevaeh thought for a second.

"Well, I'd have to tell her about you first. She's very strict about the rules."

"I hope she likes me! I can't wait to meet a real mermaid," Patricia exclaimed as she bounced in excitement.

Nevaeh laughed to herself, it seemed like Patricia was too excited to realize what she said. Arriving at the beach, they were greeted with a cool breeze, along with waves calmly crashing against the shore. Making it to the spot ahead of time, the girls sat down and talked while they waited. They talked about all sorts of things, but mainly about Nevaeh's childhood.

Struggling to hear what the girls were saying, Vavlar squinted his eyes. With no more wheat to hid in, he swiftly moved across the sand to find a spot closer to them. Finally discovering a boulder large enough, he hid behind it.

"Thanks again for saving me from that food pit," Patricia thanked Nevaeh.

"So that's where I've seen that human," Vavlar muttered to himself, "the food pit!"

Vavlar thought back to the morning he'd seen Nevaeh sneaking out, and everything began to make sense.

The girls' laughter was interrupted by the sound of a large splash coming from the water.

"Hey, what was that?" Patricia nearly jumped up from her spot.

"Don't worry, it's my mother," Nevaeh reassured her. "That's her signal to let me know she's here," she added.

Nevaeh, Patricia, and Vavlar looked towards the ocean as a woman arose from the water. Zyla began swimming closer to the shore, her tail glistening as the sun's rays bounced off of it. Not realizing Patricia was sitting there, Zyla motioned for Nevaeh to come to her. As Zyla got closer she spotted Patricia, causing her to gasp and duck down into the water. She tried to signal her daughter to not shape-shift, but it was too late.

Nevaeh had already closed her eyes, swayed back and forth, and turned into a beautiful mermaid.

"No, no, why would you shape-shift in front of this human!?" Zyla said as she rushed to the shore in a panic, "now we have to take her with us!"

"Don't worry mother, she knows what I am," Nevaeh smiled as she slid into the water.

"That doesn't make it better! How do we know we can trust her?" Zyla said, in a frustrated tone.

Patricia watched as Nevaeh and Zyla argued back and forth. Then, she had an idea.

"Watch this," Patricia said, causing both Nevaeh and Zyla to stop and look at her.

Patricia closed her eyes and began whispering something. There stood Patricia in her Deerling form.

"I have a secret of my own. I'll be sure to keep yours, too," Patricia winked.

Zyla was unsure whether or not she could truly trust Patricia, but she had no choice.

"Fine," Zyla sighed heavily, "Is there **anyone** else you've told?"

Waiting for an answer, Zyla glared at her daughter.

"Don't worry mother, she's the only one who knows," Nevaeh answered.

"Well then, I suppose we should get going," Zyla said as she wrapped her arms around Nevaeh, turning her towards the sea.

Before diving into the deep sea, Zyla took one last look at Patricia, slightly annoyed at Nevaeh's carelessness. Patricia watched the two swim off in the distance, amazed she got to meet a mermaid.

"I still can't believe it, a mermaid **and** a dragon!" Patricia muttered to herself before excitingly returning to town.

Stepping out into the open, Vavlar looks towards the ocean disgustingly.

"An outsider in our midst?" Vavlar growled, "and a slimy mermaid no less. This shall not stand."

Vavlar returned to his dragon form, enraged at this new bit of information. Taking flight, Vavlar lunges towards the volcano at top speed. The fierce winds emerging from his wings displayed how powerful his anger really was.

MEET NEVAEH AND PATRICIA!

Nevaeh

Nevaeh: designed by LPAki of DeviantArt

PATRICIA

Patricia: designed by LPAki of DeviantArt

About the Author

Frankie Williams was born in High Point, North Carolina on December 20th. In 1993 she moved to Georgia. There, she is happily married to Orlando Williams and has four amazing children.

Wanting to work with kids, and spend more time with her own, Frankie Williams opened Learning Life Childcare in 2008 - an in-home daycare.

On May 1st, 2019 her oldest daughter, Shauntae Dawkins, passed away unexpectedly. Racked with grief, Frankie remembered a conversation she had with Shauntae, who was 6-years-old at the time. She asked Shauntae what she wanted to be when she grew up, and her answer was, "a mermaid."

"This is the inspiration for *The Merdragon*," says Frankie, "and writing this story has helped me move forward."

Made in the USA
San Bernardino, CA
11 June 2020

73220534R00044